W9-BSL-186

THIRTY-TWO

AUG 2 0 2002

Song
OF
THE
Circus

Lois Duncan

Illustrated by **Meg Cundiff**

Philomel Books

This is the Circus.

This is the Man Who Wears Purple Tights,
Who gets shot from cannons
and goes on flights
To the very top of the Circus.

This is the Lady With Golden Hair,

who flies
from
a swing
and gets thrown in the air
To the Man at the Top of the Circus.

This is Gisselda, who learned to crawl
On canvas tarps, and to toss a ball
To a Fat Baboon, and who took her naps
On tattooed shoulders and spangled laps.

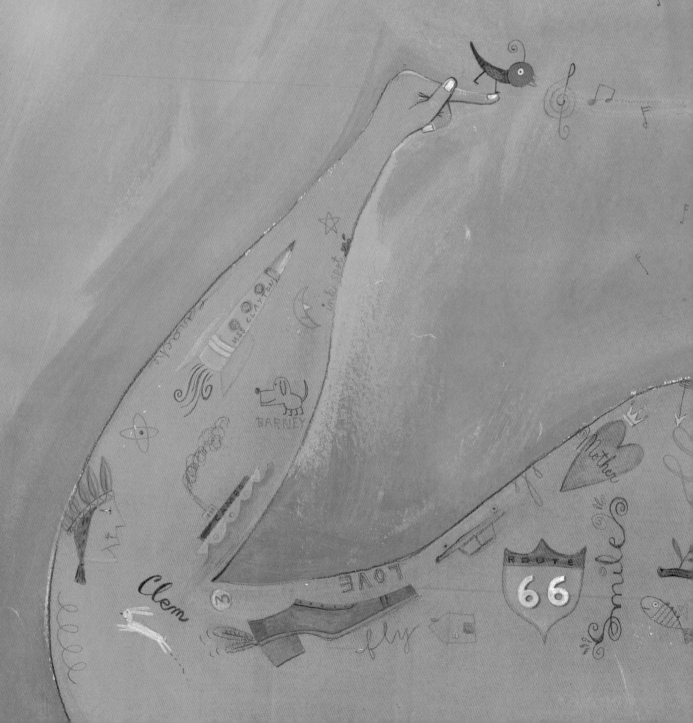

For she is a Child of the Circus.

This funny couple
named Mom and Pop
Are Bicycle Clowns,
and their son
named Bop

Is the Littlest Clown in the Circus.

This is the way
   that those children grew.
They did some things no child can do
Who doesn't belong to the Circus.

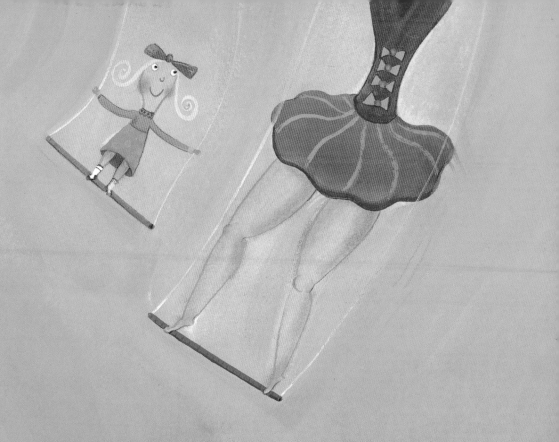

Now **don't** get scared,
    but—you see that cage?

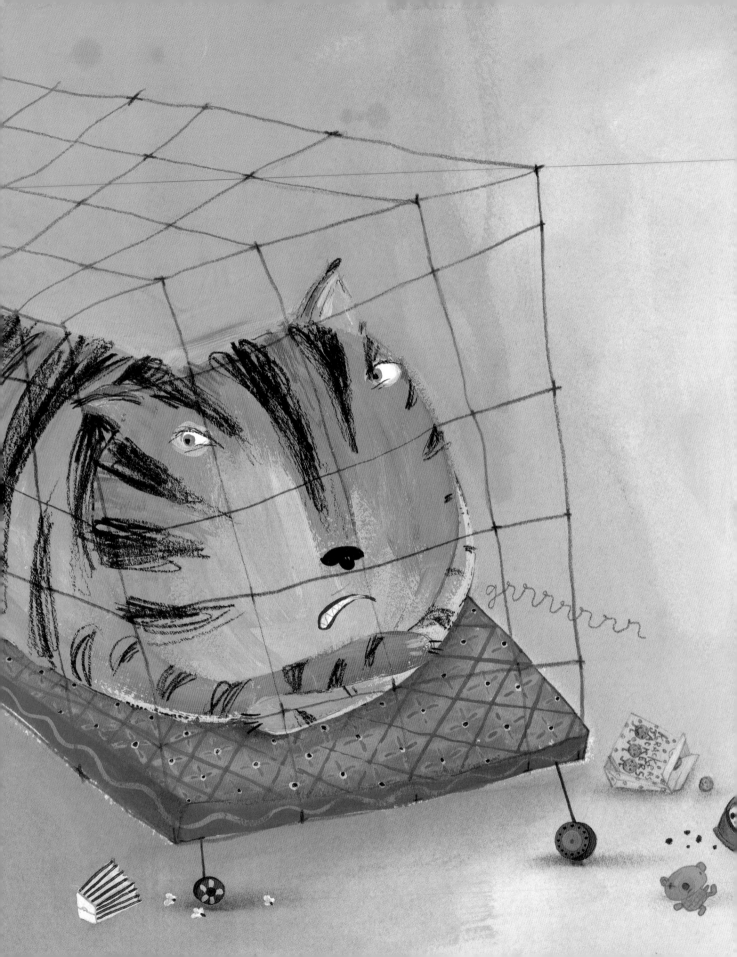

grrrrrr

And the snarling Tiger so filled with rage?
That Jungle Cat is so
mean and *wild*
That he dreams of eating a Circus Child!

(For he hates the food
at this Circus.)

On a glorious day
for the Jungle Cat

The Bicycle Clowns
had a tire go

f l a t

And, thrown from their bike
and across the ring,
They **knocked**
the Acrobats
off their swing.
The four sailed **shrieking**
through empty air
And landed on top of . . .

the Dancing Bear.

The Bear (at heart a most gentle fellow)
Threw back his head and let out a

BELLOW

That scared the Horse in the Crimson Capes,

Who pulled a cart filled with Gibbering Apes.

The wagon crashed and broke into sections,

With Monkeys scampering in all directions.

The rest of the Horses reared in their tracks

And Bareback Riders flew off their backs,

With one of them doing a loop-the-loop

To land in a pile of Elephant poop.

(There's a lot of that at the Circus.)

The Elephants went on a grand stampede,
The Fat Lady's Elephant in the lead.
The Fat Lady screamed and went pale with dread,
For she saw to her horror what lay ahead—
The most frightening
thing at the
Circus!

The Elephant crashed
with an awful **THUD**

(With bumps and bruises, though not much blood)—

But the cage was shattered,
the Tiger OUT!

He bared his teeth
as he whirled about.

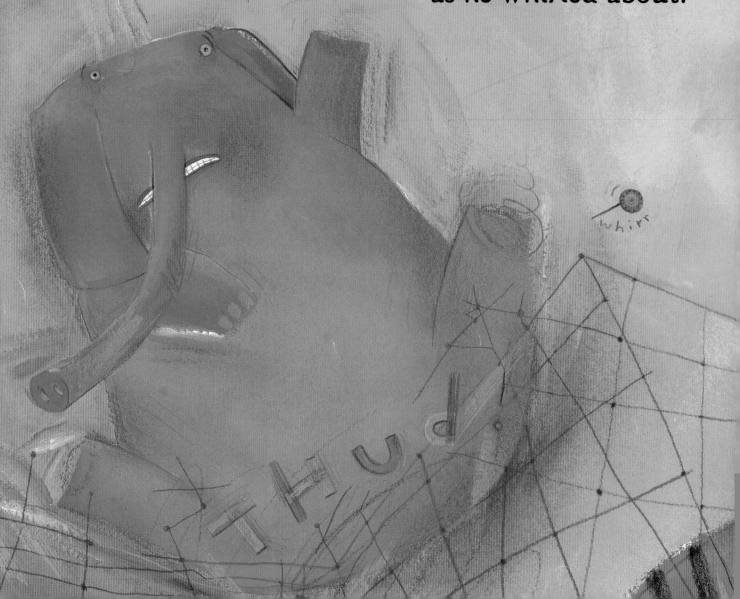

The Fat Lady lay in a quivering heap,
But the Tiger passed her with one great leap.
That lucky lady had no appeal—

What he had in mind
was a lighter meal.

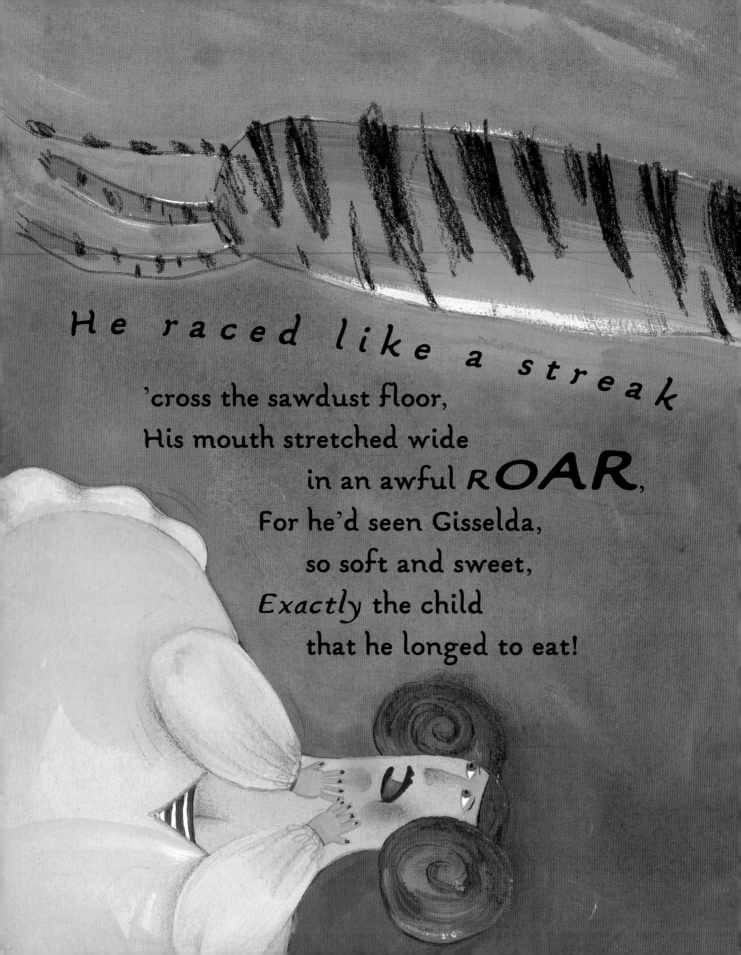

He raced like a streak
'cross the sawdust floor,
His mouth stretched wide
in an awful ROAR,
For he'd seen Gisselda,
so soft and sweet,
Exactly the child
that he longed to eat!

What a terrible day at the Circus!

But Bop came running.
He shouted,
"NO!
Don't eat that girl!
She needs time to grow!"

The Tiger whirled
and leapt straight for Bop,
And 'twas small Gisselda
who hollered,

"STOP!"

Those two brave children
stood staunch and tough
And screamed at the Jungle Cat,

"That's enough!

You've got to live by Circus laws.
You can't eat children, so

SHUT YOUR JAWS!"

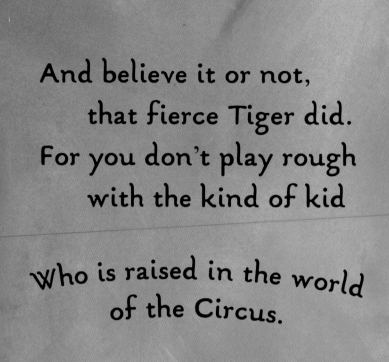

And believe it or not,
that fierce Tiger did.
For you don't play rough
with the kind of kid

Who is raised in the world
of the Circus.

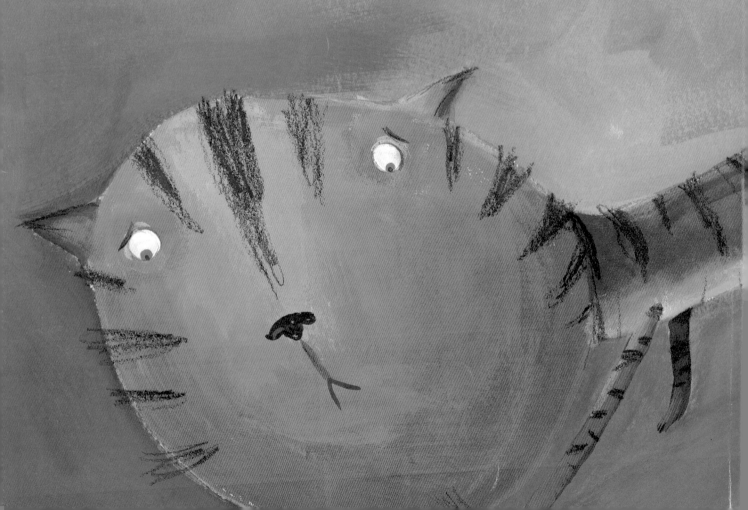

The Tiger slunk
    from the center ring
Without having dined
    on a single thing.
Bop and Gisselda
    stood hand in hand
And bowed and waved to the crowded stand.

How the people **cheered!**
For they didn't know
That the act wasn't part
of the normal show.

(You expect such things
at a Circus.)

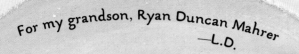

For my grandson, Ryan Duncan Mahrer
—L.D.

For little Cameron, who flies through the air
with the greatest of ease
—M.C.

Text copyright © 2002 by Lois Duncan
Illustrations copyright © 2002 by Meg Cundiff
All rights reserved. This book, or parts thereof, may not be reproduced
in any form without permission in writing from the publisher, Philomel Books,
a division of Penguin Putnam Books for Young Readers, 345 Hudson Street, New York,
NY 10014. Philomel Books, Reg. U.S. Pat. & Tm. Off. Published simultaneously in Canada.
Printed in Hong Kong by South China Printing Co. (1988) Ltd. Book design by Gina DiMassi.
The text is set in Gararond. The art was done in gouache.
Library of Congress Cataloging-in-Publication Data Duncan, Lois, 1934–   Song of the circus / Lois
Duncan; illustrated by Meg Cundiff.   Summary: Gisselda and Bop, true children of the circus, stand
up to the snarling tiger on the terrible day that the whole performance goes wrong.
[1. Circus—Fiction. 2. Tigers—Fiction. 3. Stories in rhyme.] I. Cundiff, Meg Michele, 1959– ill. II. Title.
PZ8.3.D9158 So 2002 [E]—dc21 00-023139 ISBN 0-399-23397-0
1 3 5 7 9 10 8 6 4 2
First Impression

How the people **cheered!**
For they didn't know
That the act wasn't part
of the normal show.

(You expect such things
at a Circus.)

For my grandson, Ryan Duncan Mahrer
—L.D.

For little Cameron, who flies through the air
with the greatest of ease
—M.C.

Text copyright © 2002 by Lois Duncan
Illustrations copyright © 2002 by Meg Cundiff

a division of Penguin Putnam Books for Young Readers, 345 Hudson Street, New York,
NY 10014. Philomel Books, Reg. U.S. Pat. & Tm. Off. Published simultaneously in Canada.
Printed in Hong Kong by South China Printing Co. (1988) Ltd. Book design by Gina DiMassi.
The text is set in Gararond. The art was done in gouache.
Library of Congress Cataloging-in-Publication Data Duncan, Lois, 1934—   Song of the circus / Lois
Duncan; illustrated by Meg Cundiff.   Summary: Gisselda and Bop, true children of the circus, stand
up to the snarling tiger on the terrible day that the whole performance goes wrong.
[1. Circus—Fiction. 2. Tigers—Fiction. 3. Stories in rhyme.] I. Cundiff, Meg Michele, 1959— ill. II. Title.
PZ8.3.D9158 So 2002 [E]—dc21 00-023139 ISBN 0-399-23397-0
1 3 5 7 9 10 8 6 4 2
First Impression